A NOTE TO PARENTS

Reading Aloud with Your Child

Research shows that reading books aloud is the single most valuable support parents can provide in helping children learn to read.

- Be a ham! The more enthusiasm you display, the more your child will enjoy the book.
- Run your finger underneath the words as you read to signal that the print carries the story.
- Leave time for examining the illustrations more closely; encourage your child to find things in the pictures.
- Invite your youngster to join in whenever there's a repeated phrase in the text.
- Link up events in the book with similar events in your child's life.
- If your child asks a question, stop and answer it. The book can be a means to learning more about your child's thoughts.

Listening to Your Child Read Aloud

The support of your attention and praise is absolutely crucial to your child's continuing efforts to learn to read.

- If your child is learning to read and asks for a word, give it immediately so that the meaning of the story is not interrupted. DO NOT ask your child to sound out the word.
- On the other hand, if your child initiates the act of sounding out, don't intervene.
- If your child is reading along and makes what is called a miscue, listen for the sense of the miscue. If the word "road" is substituted for the word "street," for instance, no meaning is lost. Don't stop the reading for a correction.
- If the miscue makes no sense (for example, "horse" for "house"), ask your child to reread the sentence because you're not sure you understand what's just been read.
- Above all else, enjoy your child's growing command of print and make sure you give lots of praise. *You are your child's first teacher—and the most important one. Praise from you is critical for further risk-taking and learning.*

—Priscilla Lynch
Ph.D., New York University
Educational Consultant

D0011061

Library of Congress Cataloging-in-Publication Data

Brownrigg, Sheri.
    Best friends wear pink tutus / by Sheri Brownrigg ; illustrated by Meredith Johnson.
        p.   cm. — (Hello reader)
    Summary: When two friends vie for a part in "The Nutcracker," who will get the part?
    ISBN 0-590-46437-X
    [1. Ballet dancing—Fiction. 2. Friendship—Fiction.] I. Johnson, Meredith, ill. II. Title. III. Series.
PZ7.B8243Be   1993
[E]—dc20   92-27569
                                                               CIP
                                                                AC

12   11   10   9   8   7   6   5   4   3   2   1   3   4   5   6   7   8/9

                    Printed in the U.S.A.   23

            First Scholastic printing, September 1993

BEST FRIENDS
Wear
Pink Tutus

by Sheri Brownrigg
Illustrated by Meredith Johnson

Hello Reader!—Level 2

SCHOLASTIC INC.

New York   Toronto   London   Auckland   Sydney

I'm Amanda,
and this is Emily.

We're best friends,
and we wear pink tutus.

We wear pink tutus to school.

We wear pink tutus to the store.

We even wear pink tutus
to go roller skating.

Best of all, we wear
our pink tutus to ballet class.

Our ballet class is going
to dance *The Nutcracker*.

Each student will try out for a part.
Our teacher, Miss Yvonne,
will decide who gets it.

I want to be Marie.
So does Emily.

"I really want to be Marie," Emily says.
"But I really want to be Marie," I say.

If I get to be Marie, then Emily will be sad, and that will make me sad.

If Emily gets to be Marie, then I will be sad, and that will make Emily sad.

Marie doesn't get to wear a pink tutu,
but she is the star of the show.

Miss Yvonne says
there can only be one Marie.

"Sometimes being your best friend is hard," Emily says.

For the tryouts, we decide not
to be best friends.

We warm up at opposite sides of the
room. We try not to look at each
other.

"Pretend you are Marie and show me how you would dance for your new Nutcracker doll," Miss Yvonne says.

Emily is dancing very well.
I think she may get the part.

Suddenly she sees me.

Emily acts dizzy and wobbles.

That's odd. Spinning never made
her dizzy before.

Now it's my turn. I point my toes
like a real ballerina.

Then I see Emily. I kick the doll over on purpose.

Oops! It's not time for the Nutcracker to lose his head yet!

Miss Yvonne picks Nicole to be Marie.
Nicole is an older girl.

"Amanda and Emily will be snowflakes in 'The Snowflake Waltz,'" says Miss Yvonne.

"Together?" I ask.

"Of course," says Miss Yvonne.

Miss Yvonne knows we dance better together.

And we know we dance better
when we are best friends.

Anyway, we would rather be snowflakes.
Snowflakes get to wear tutus.

I guess we are the first *pink* snowflakes
in the history of *The Nutcracker*!